THE PURPLE PUFFY COAT

Maribeth Boelts

illustrated by Daniel Duncan

WALKER BOOKS
AND SUBSIDIARIES

LONDON · BOSTON · SYDNEY · AUCKLAND

To Nouran, who gives the perfect gifts,
and who is one herself. With love always.
MB

First published 2020 by Walker Books Ltd, 87 Vauxhall Walk, London SE11 5HJ • Text © 2020 Maribeth Boelts
Illustrations © 2020 Daniel Duncan • The right of Maribeth Boelts and Daniel Duncan to be identified as author and
illustrator respectively of this work has been asserted by them in accordance with the Copyright, Designs and Patents Act
1988 • This book has been typeset in Aunt Mildred • Printed in China • All rights reserved. No part of this book may be
reproduced, transmitted or stored in an information retrieval system in any form or by any means, graphic, electronic
or mechanical, including photocopying, taping and recording, without prior written permission from the publisher.
British Library Cataloguing in Publication Data: a catalogue record for this book is available from the British Library
ISBN 978-1-4063-9205-0 • www.walker.co.uk • 10 9 8 7 6 5 4 3 2 1

Beetle and Stick Insect walked home from the bus stop, shivering in the cold wind.

"Stick Insect, it's November. That means your birthday is almost here," said Beetle.

"You're right," said Stick Insect. "Just seven more days."

"Well," said Beetle, "I already have your present, because that's just the kind of friend I am. Always thinking of everyone else."

"That's true," said Stick Insect.

"But how can I wait seven days? Your present is SO amazing, and you need it SO much – I must give it to you early," said Beetle.

Beetle scurried inside his apartment, and Stick Insect followed.

Beetle handed Stick Insect a big box.

Stick Insect removed the lid. He stared.

"IT'S A PURPLE PUFFY COAT!" said Beetle. "Isn't it breathtaking?"

"It does look ... warm," said Stick Insect. "And purple is your favourite colour. Thank you, Beetle."

"Try it on! Try it on!" said Beetle.

"You mean now?" said Stick Insect.

"Yes, now!" said Beetle.

Stick Insect encased himself in the purple puffy coat. He looked in the mirror.

"It's showy, isn't it?" said Stick Insect.

"Showy and *glorious!*" gushed Beetle.
"We must strut about."

Beetle and Stick Insect walked through the neighbourhood.

"Everyone is staring," whispered Stick Insect.

"Did you see they're pointing too?" said Beetle. "They're wondering where they might get a fancy coat like yours. They're wondering if you bought it yourself or if someone generous and thoughtful gave it to you as a gift."

"You're sure?" said Stick Insect.

"I'm sure," said Beetle. "I'll go and chat with them."

While Beetle boasted and bragged, Stick Insect waited.

He waited behind a tree,

inside a pile of leaves

and under a bench.

"Silly Stick Insect," said Beetle. "Come out and be the *centre of attention!*"

Stick Insect shuddered.

"I know just what you need," said Beetle. "Every day, we'll have an outing in your purple puffy coat so you can get used to being a spectacle."

Beetle and Stick Insect visited the library,

the supermarket

and the skate park, with Beetle admiring the purple coat at every turn.

It was the night before Stick Insect's birthday. "I already gave Stick Insect his purple puffy coat," said Beetle. "I'll paint his portrait as another gift."

Beetle sketched and painted.

"I've finished everything but his face," said Beetle. "First, I will try to remember how Stick Insect looks whenever he is wearing his purple puffy coat."

Beetle sketched a huge smile on Stick Insect's face.

"Hmmm," said Beetle. "He doesn't look quite like that."

He sketched a medium-sized smile.

"That's not him either," said Beetle.

Then he sketched no smile at all.

Beetle stared at Stick Insect's purple puffy ... *glumness*.

"OH, NO!" wailed Beetle. "That is *exactly* how Stick Insect looks every time he is wearing his purple puffy coat!"

Beetle dashed to the shop.

"I'll get Stick Insect a different coat!"
he said.

PUFFY COAT BOUTIQUE

Open

"A rainbow puffy coat! A sparkly puffy coat!
A polka-dotted puffy coat!"

Then Beetle stopped.

He thought hard about Stick Insect.

Who Stick Insect was – and who he was *not*.

When the sun came up, Beetle knocked on Stick Insect's door, carrying one teeny-tiny present.

"HAPPY BIRTHDAY, STICK INSECT!" shouted Beetle.

"Thank you, Beetle!" said Stick Insect.

"I have something for you," said Beetle.

Stick Insect unwrapped the teeny-tiny box.

He opened the note inside, and read it aloud.

You never need to wear your purple puffy coat ever again.
Your Friend
Beetle x

"Oh, Beetle!" cried Stick Insect. "Are you certain? You love my purple puffy coat!"

"I do, but you do not, Stick Insect," said Beetle. "And I want you to be happy."

Stick Insect gave Beetle a hug. "Then you couldn't have given me a better present," he said. "Now, wait here."

Stick Insect opened his wardrobe. He brought out his purple puffy coat.

"I want you to be happy too, Beetle," said Stick Insect. "The purple puffy coat is yours."

"REALLY?" said Beetle.

"Yes, really," said Stick Insect. "Try it on."

Beetle tried it on.

"Too long and too baggy," said Stick Insect.
"I'll fix that right up."

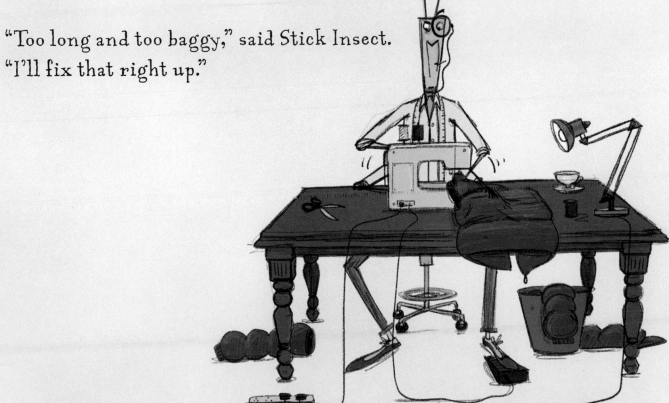

"A purple puffy VEST!" said Beetle. "How do I look, Stick Insect?"

"*Magnificent!*" said Stick Insect. "And how do I look, Beetle?"

"Like my *VERY* happy friend on his birthday!" said Beetle.